EVERY BEAT OF

MY HEART

~ The Sullivans ~

Wedding Novella

Bella Andre

EVERY BEAT OF MY HEART

~ The Sullivans ~

Wedding Novella

© 2016 Bella Andre

Sign up for Bella's New Release Newsletter

http://www.bellaandre.com/newsletter

www.BellaAndre.com

Bella on Twitter: @bellaandre

Bella on Facebook: facebook.com/bellaandrefans

bella@bellaandre.com

"You are cordially invited to a very special wedding..."

What do you get when two Sullivans pick the same wedding date?

Two super-sexy grooms.

Two beautiful brides.

Two very unconventional (four-legged and furry) ring bearers.

And Sullivans from around the word coming together to celebrate vows of forever with auto mogul Zach Sullivan and dog trainer Heather Linsey—and pro baseball star Ryan Sullivan and sculptor Vicki Bennett.

This is the double wedding millions of Sullivan fans have been waiting for...

Special note from Bella Andre: If you are already a fan of the series, I hope you absolutely love being able to reconnect with all your favorite San Francisco and Seattle Sullivans! If you are just getting started, this is a great way to meet everyone, and you can find a Sullivan Family Tree on my website (bellaandre.com/sullivan-family-tree).

A note from Bella

Over the past five years, countless readers have written to ask if I could write a story about how your favorite Sullivans are doing. I am beyond thrilled to finally fulfill that request—especially given that writing *EVERY BEAT OF MY HEART* has been such a wonderful experience. I've laughed and cried along with each and every one of my heroes and heroines as they worked together to put on this fun and emotional wedding.

If you are already a fan of the series, I hope you love being able to reconnect with all your favorite San Francisco and Seattle Sullivans! If you are just getting started, this is a great way to meet everyone. You can find out how Zach and Heather first found love in *IF YOU WERE MINE* and learn more about Ryan and Vicki's love story in *LET ME BE THE ONE*.

One other frequent request has been for a family tree, and I'm very pleased to include one in this book. You can also find it on my website: www.BellaAndre.com/Sullivan-Family-Tree

Last, but certainly not least, I want to thank you for reading my books and for writing me such lovely emails and online comments. Knowing that you love my Sullivans as much as I do makes me very, very happy!

Happy reading,
Bella Andre

PS: After writing more than a dozen books about the Sullivan family, I'm always amazed to find myself falling more in love with them than ever. Now that the San Francisco and Seattle Sullivans have all found love, it's time for their cousins in New York and Maine to find love too! Drake Sullivan kicks off the New York branch with *NOW THAT I'VE FOUND YOU* and his sister, Suzanne, will be next in *SINCE I FELL FOR YOU*!

PPS: As a special bonus, I've put together a behind-the-scenes look at what inspired me to first write about the Sullivans—and why I plan to keep writing about them for as long as I possibly can! Click on the image below to find out more or visit www.BellaAndre.com/secret

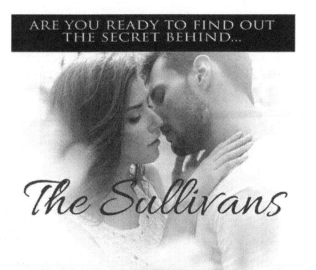

ARE YOU READY TO FIND OUT
THE SECRET BEHIND...

The Sullivans

WWW.BELLAANDRE.COM/SECRET

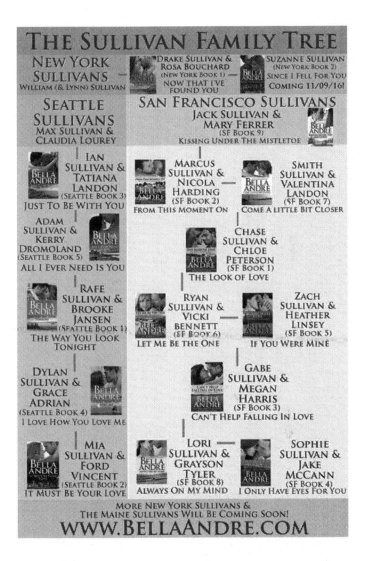

THE SULLIVAN FAMILY TREE

NEW YORK SULLIVANS — William (& Lynn) Sullivan

Drake Sullivan & Rosa Bouchard (New York Book 1) — NOW THAT I'VE FOUND YOU

Suzanne Sullivan (New York Book 2) — SINCE I FELL FOR YOU — Coming 11/09/16!

SEATTLE SULLIVANS

Max Sullivan & Claudia Lourey

SAN FRANCISCO SULLIVANS

Jack Sullivan & Mary Ferrer (SF Book 9) — KISSING UNDER THE MISTLETOE

Ian Sullivan & Tatiana Landon (Seattle Book 3) — JUST TO BE WITH YOU

Marcus Sullivan & Nicola Harding (SF Book 2) — FROM THIS MOMENT ON

Smith Sullivan & Valentina Landon (SF Book 7) — COME A LITTLE BIT CLOSER

Adam Sullivan & Kerry Dromoland (Seattle Book 5) — ALL I EVER NEED IS YOU

Chase Sullivan & Chloe Peterson (SF Book 1) — THE LOOK OF LOVE

Rafe Sullivan & Brooke Jansen (Seattle Book 1) — THE WAY YOU LOOK TONIGHT

Ryan Sullivan & Vicki Bennett (SF Book 6) — LET ME BE THE ONE

Zach Sullivan & Heather Linsey (SF Book 5) — IF YOU WERE MINE

Dylan Sullivan & Grace Adrian (Seattle Book 4) — I LOVE HOW YOU LOVE ME

Gabe Sullivan & Megan Harris (SF Book 3) — CAN'T HELP FALLING IN LOVE

Mia Sullivan & Ford Vincent (Seattle Book 2) — IT MUST BE YOUR LOVE

Lori Sullivan & Grayson Tyler (SF Book 8) — ALWAYS ON MY MIND

Sophie Sullivan & Jake McCann (SF Book 4) — I ONLY HAVE EYES FOR YOU

MORE NEW YORK SULLIVANS &
THE MAINE SULLIVANS WILL BE COMING SOON!

WWW.BELLAANDRE.COM

CHAPTER ONE

The dogs gave away Heather Linsey's appearance a full sixty seconds before she walked into Zach Sullivan's garage. Cuddles and Atlas ran in to greet Zach at top speed, the tags on their collars clinking and clanging like wind chimes. Though Atlas weighed a hundred and fifty pounds more than Cuddles, he had enough control over his big, long limbs to stop himself before he hit the classic—and priceless—1974 Ferrari 365 GT4 that Zach was working on. Cuddles, on the other hand, though barely eight pounds soaking wet, went sliding all the way beneath the car.

"Goofballs." Zach looked at Atlas. "Want me to get your girlfriend out from under there?" He could have sworn the Great Dane nodded.

Both of them bent down to look for the teacup Yorkie under the car. And as Cuddles sat just out of reach with her tail wagging a million miles an hour and her tongue hanging out of her mouth, Zach was reminded of the first time he met Heather, right here at

Sullivan Autos.

Best day of his life.

"Nothing wrong with that view," she said a few moments later in a voice laced with humor and more than a little sensuality.

The sound of Heather's voice was all it took to rev Zach's engine. Grinning, with his torso still under the car, he did a mini-twerk for her.

Her laughter warmed every cell in his body as she walked over to the side of the car and said, "Be still, my heart." Making his fiancée laugh was one of Zach's number one goals in life. She'd been too serious for too long before they found each other.

Hearing Heather's voice, Cuddles clearly decided it would be more fun to be with her than to keep toying with Zach and Atlas. With a doggy grin, she trotted out from under the car, and Zach immediately scooped her up.

With the dog tucked under one arm, Zach stood up, then pulled his fiancée against him. "You stole my line." Her mouth was warm and sweet beneath his as he kissed her, then said, "My heart hasn't beat normally since the first day you walked into my garage and gave me hell."

The truth was, he'd never expected a woman like Heather to come into his life. Sparks had jumped between them from the first, and when they finally gave in to their feelings for each other? *Explosion* wasn't anywhere near a good enough word for the heat of their lovemaking.

The most amazing thing of all, however, wasn't just that he'd found her in the first place. It was that life with her just kept getting better and better.

"You were so hot," she muttered in a voice made slightly breathless from his kiss, "and so infuriatingly cocky."

"And now?"

"You're still hot." She grinned. "And just as cocky as ever."

"You love it."

"I love you," she clarified. "So I put up with the rest of the package."

"Speaking of the rest of the package—" Her mouth was too tempting to resist kissing again. "—want to get kinky in the backseat of a souped-up Ferrari?"

She raised an eyebrow. "Is that why you asked me to leave my office to visit you in the middle of the day?"

"Would that be a problem if it was?"

She slid her hands under his shirt, and his abdominal muscles flexed and jumped as she replied with a cocky grin of her own, "It will only be a problem if you take more than sixty seconds to get my clothes off."

"Don't start counting yet."

"Too late." Her wicked smile made his heart jump so fast and hard inside his chest that he could practically hear it reverberating against the walls and concrete floor. "One. Two. Three."

Zach carefully put Cuddles down, told both dogs to go lie on their dog beds in the corner, then went to hit the button on the wall that closed his garage doors. After locking the door that led to his office as well, he sprinted back to Heather, who was at *ten* by then.

He didn't bother with undoing buttons, just tore her shirt open and shoved it off. They had a change of outfits for her in his locker, just in case something like this should happen to her clothes. Which it did. Often.

She gasped at his caveman approach, but he could tell by the way her pupils dilated that she loved it just as much as he did. Otherwise, why would she have given him a running time clock?

Her countdown grew huskier with every second that passed. He'd never thought the word *nineteen* could sound sexy, but boy, did it ever.

Her bra came next, but since it was one of his favorites—a pink and white lacy thing from which her breasts spilled in the sexiest possible way—he unclipped the front latch before sliding it off her shoulders rather than ripping it in two.

"Thirty-one." She licked her lips, the tip of her

tongue wetting that gorgeous mouth of hers. "And you've still got so much to take off."

Sweet Lord, he loved the way they teased. Sparred *and* sparked. He could spend a thousand years with Heather and never feel bored. Never wish that he could have anyone else. Not when Heather was absolutely *everything* to him.

"Don't worry," he promised, "you'll be naked and in the backseat before sixty."

Without giving her any warning, he picked her up and had her on the leather seat by *thirty-nine.* His mouth was watering at the way her breasts were bouncing from the trip into the car, but he couldn't let himself be distracted. Not yet. Not until he had her jeans and panties off too.

Thankfully, she was hungry enough for him that she was already kicking off her shoes by the time he'd unbuttoned and unzipped her jeans.

"Fifty-one."

He grinned, deciding to take every last one of the remaining nine seconds to tease them both by slowly sliding denim and lace down her long, toned legs. Her voice shook with each of the final seconds she spoke aloud, and he wondered just how close she was to begging by now. By his estimation, not far at all.

He muffled *sixty* with his mouth on hers and his hands in her hair as he freed the long, silky strands from her braid. And when she wrapped her gorgeous naked limbs all around him and pulled him down over her on the backseat, every last one of his teenage dreams came true. Again.

He was running kisses over the soft skin of her neck and shoulders when she said, "You really are good at that."

"Never say I don't have at least one worthwhile skill."

"One *really* worthwhile skill." She reached for his shirt and pulled it up over his head, then put her hands flat on his bare chest and stared at him with unabashed hunger. "You really are nice to look at too."

Sliding one hand up her torso so that he could cup one breast, he looked into her brown eyes that were flecked with gold and at her rosy mouth that always tempted him beyond reason. "Ditto."

"And so romantic," she added, but she was smiling as she said it.

"I knew I should have given you the bouquet of flowers I bought for you before taking your clothes off."

Though she lit up knowing that he'd gotten her flowers, she shook her head. "No way. Clothes off first, flowers second is just right."

Just right. That's what Zach and Heather were for each other. Both in—and out—of bed. Or, as the case currently was, in the back of a very expensive race car.

He lowered his mouth to her breast just as she reached for his belt. But as he laved her sensitive flesh in just the way he knew made her crazy, instead of undoing his belt, she gripped it for dear life.

"How do you always do that? Touch me so perfectly every single time?"

He licked over her again, then bit down lightly on the taut peak with the edge of his teeth, making her shiver with need before he replied, "Because I love you."

"I love you t—*ohhhh.*"

Desperation spun her words out into unintelligible sounds as he traced his fingertips lightly between her thighs. She was already so wet. So damned hot. So *ready*.

"I can't wait another second, Heather. I need to feel you, need to taste you." Even as he slid his fingers over her drenched sex, he was kissing his way down her body, using his tongue and lips and teeth to drive her higher and higher. So high that the very second he found the center of her arousal with the tip of his tongue, she blasted off into ecstasy.

God, he loved the way she tasted. Loved the way she held nothing back as she trembled and moaned and begged him for more, her long hair a silky tangle on the leather backseat. She was still floating in pleasure when he came back up over her, his clothes off now too.

"How the hell did I ever get this lucky?" He'd asked her this question a million times during the past three years—and he knew he'd be asking it forever.

She opened her eyes and smiled at him. "I'm pretty sure you owe it all to Summer, Gabe, and Megan."

Zach's brother Gabe, his wife, and their daughter had brought Cuddles to Zach as a puppy. Summer had said she knew the minute she met the tiny little dog that she was meant to be Zach's. They'd needed a dog trainer, and Heather was the best in the city. When Cuddles and Heather's dog, Atlas, fell in love at first sight, the dogs had wanted to spend every second together—which meant Heather and Zach had become really close, really fast.

He'd never thought he would meet a woman like her. A woman who was not only his match—but who bested him in every single category. Looks. Swagger. Humor.

It was only when it came to *love* that they were equals.

"I love you, Heather."

He moved to take her, but she was already there, meeting him halfway. Right from the start, Heather's body had fit his like no other. But now that they knew each other's rhythms and pleasures so intimately, he could barely rein himself in to make sure she peaked again before he lost it completely.

As if she could read his mind, she put her hands on his face and kissed him. "I love you, too." She wriggled out from under him and began to turn over. "Especially when you lose control." His brain nearly stuttered to a halt as she went on her hands and knees on the supple leather of the backseat. "When you *take* control."

He was inside of her again before either of them could take their next breath, hauling her up against him, one hand between her legs, the other on her breasts. Their lovemaking was always beyond hot, but the way they were taking each other today was animal. *Feral.*

"Now." He urged her with his hands over her breasts, which seemed even fuller than usual. They were definitely more sensitive as he rolled the gorgeous peaks between his thumbs and middle fingers until her hips were bucking even harder against his. "Come apart for me, Heather. I want to feel you. I *need* to feel you."

The words had barely fallen from his lips before she exploded in a climax so powerful that it took Zach closer to paradise than he'd ever been before. Having the strongest, most incredible woman in the world come apart in his arms was a gift he'd never, ever take for granted.

Once his heart was beating at a halfway normal speed again, he shifted them on the backseat so that she was lying on her back looking up at him and he was levered up on one arm. He reached out to slide a lock of damp hair away from her forehead. "Want to know the other reason I asked you to come by today?"

"You really had another reason?"

He would have smiled, but he needed her to know how serious he was as he said, "I want you to be mine, Heather."

A small frown line formed between her brows. "I already am."

"You're my fiancée. But I want you to be my wife. And I want to be your husband. Not in another year from now. Not in six months. As soon as possible."

"I want that too." Her voice was soft but sure. As sure as he felt about spending forever together. "If I know you—which I think I do, better than anyone else, by now—you've not only got a date in mind, you've already booked the details."

It was true. No one had ever known him as well as Heather. She'd broken through all his walls, shown him that love was more important than anything else. "November fifteenth."

He'd expected her to look surprised, stunned even. But she simply raised one eyebrow and said, "You really think we can get everything and everyone together for a wedding in two weeks?"

"Worst case, we'll hop a flight to Vegas and get Elvis to marry us."

"You'd love that, wouldn't you?" she said with a laugh.

"You, me, and Elvis with Huge and Tiny as our witnesses?" He grinned. "Sounds like a pretty damn epic wedding to me."

"Yes. Not to Elvis," she clarified before he could get carried away with his grand Vegas plans, "but to getting married in two weeks."

The first time she'd said *yes* had been when she'd agreed to a sex-only fling with him three years ago. When they'd both tumbled head over heels in love with each other, her next *yes* had been after his marriage proposal. This *yes*, to their wedding date, felt just as big.

Just like every other time, he sealed her *yes* with a kiss, but this time he also took her hands and threaded his fingers through hers. "Every time your fingers slide between mine, I remember lying with you at the park in San Francisco, holding your hand, and never wanting to let go."

"I didn't want you to let go either. Not then. Not now. Not ever." But instead of smiling as she said it, he could see tears forming in her eyes. "I know I was teasing you about being romantic before, but you really are."

"Heather? What's wrong?" Whatever it was, he would fix it.

"Nothing." She wrapped her arms and legs even tighter around him. "Absolutely nothing's wrong."

His heart pounding, he forced himself to simply stroke her hair and then her back, rather than keep pushing her to tell him what was going on. Heather was the strongest woman he'd ever met. He'd broken all his rules for her. Had fallen in love hard and fast even when he'd sworn he never would. And she'd broken her rules about love for him too. There was nothing they wouldn't do for each other, no fear they wouldn't share, no joy they wouldn't celebrate. She'd tell him more when she was ready.

Finally, she settled back and gazed up at him. "When you asked me to come by the garage, I was actually already planning to." She tried to take a deep breath, but it shuddered in her chest. "I took a test this morning at work." She looked into his eyes. "I'm pregnant."

Everything inside Zach's brain went blank, and he swore his heart actually stopped beating for a split second before blood came rushing in like a flash flood. All he could do was echo her words. "You're pregnant?"

"Yes." The word shook slightly in her throat. "We're going to have a baby."

He could hardly breathe. Could hardly think a coherent thought. All he could do was kiss Heather and pull her tight against him.

"A baby." His eyes were wet now too. "We're going to have a kid. A little bruiser like me or a beauty like you." He had to put his mouth on hers again, had to say to her with his kisses all the things he couldn't yet form into words. "You hear that Atlas? Cuddles?" he said as he tugged her naked from the car a few moments later. "You're going to have a brother or sister to play with and protect soon."

As if the dogs could actually understand what he was saying—and were as thrilled about it as he was—they ran up to Heather and Zach with tails wagging.

She was laughing as she patted the dogs on the head, then reached for her clothes. "You tore my shirt again." She shook her head while she slipped back into her bra and panties. "Good thing I love you. All three of you," she said as the dogs started to roll into a spot of axle grease on the concrete floor. "Nice Ferrari, by the way."

Unable to be apart from her for more than a few seconds, especially today when she'd just made him the happiest guy alive all over again, he had to pull her back into his arms as soon as they both had their clothes on. He had been planning to sell the sports car, but that was before Heather had given him the greatest news in the world in its backseat.

"I'm going to keep it."

"I was hoping you'd say that." She took his hand and drew him back toward the car. "Turns out it's true what they say about pregnant women's libidos."

She always took him from zero to a hundred in a matter of seconds. But knowing he had nine months ahead of him with Heather wanting to jump him in—and out—of this backseat? And that at the end of that, they'd have a new baby to love?

Once upon a time, he hadn't believed it was possible for him to ever be this lucky. But he was.

All because of Heather.

CHAPTER TWO

I need you. Come quick.

Ryan Sullivan was standing in the Hawks locker room with nothing but a towel wrapped around his waist post-shower when Vicki Bennett's text came. Once upon a time, seeing this text from her would have sent terror into his heart. But today he grinned like a fool instead.

He'd just finished pitching practice, followed by a workout in the weight room—and had been called out by both his coach and his trainer for his inattention. The first World Series game was in only a handful of days, and Ryan's face was currently on the cover of *Sports Illustrated*, along with the headline: "Can the Greatest Pitcher in Major League Baseball History Do It Again?" He understood why his team wanted him one hundred percent focused on the game—but he wouldn't apologize for missing his fiancée, damn it. Vicki had been working in France for the past two weeks, and it irritated him beyond measure that instead of being there to welcome her home this morning after her overnight flight, he'd had to be at the stadium.

He couldn't have been happier about her growing notoriety as a sculptor, and he would never begrudge her the time she wanted to spend in her studio creating beautiful art. Just as she would never want him to feel guilty for the hours he spent with his team for practices and games. But it was still frustrating as hell that between their two busy schedules, the only moments they could grab together lately were stolen ones.

Ryan had fallen for Vicki after she moved to Palo Alto when they were fifteen years old and they'd instantly become friends. But before he could get up the nerve to tell her that his feelings went way past friendship, her father had been transferred to the East Coast. Ryan never forgot her, though, not even after she married another guy after graduating from college, and moved to Europe. He never stopped loving her either. So the day three years ago when she'd texted asking him to come quick and help her deal with a creepy "mentor" who was hitting on her in a bar, he'd dropped everything and raced there as fast as he could. They'd ended up having to fake not only a relationship, but an engagement as well. Thankfully, before long there was nothing fake at all about their relationship. Not only were they still best friends, but the passion between them burned hotter than anything Ryan had ever imagined possible.

Thank God pretend engagements—and unrequited love where the two of them circled each other while secretly wishing for so much more—were old news now. This morning, he'd arranged to have three dozen flowers sent over to her studio to celebrate the three years they'd been together.

Figuring she must be texting because she'd received the flowers, he put on his clothes in record time and was heading out when the new pitching coach, Stuart, walked in.

"You're looking happier now. Let me guess—you're going home to see the wife?"

Ryan's grin faltered. He and Vicki kept meaning to figure out a date for their wedding, but whenever they were able to find time to be together, opening up calendars and scanning through schedules was the last thing either of them wanted to do. He was *this close* to hauling her over his shoulder into City Hall and just getting the deed done.

Everyone always thought things came so easily to Ryan. But right now he missed Vicki so much he couldn't see straight—let alone throw a ball worth a damn.

It was true that he hadn't had to fight for much in his life, but he'd had to fight for her three years ago when she'd told him that she thought going from best friends to lovers was a mistake. Even now that they were deeply in love and committed to each other, he'd never stop fighting for her.

"Good guess," he said, deciding not to correct his coach over the difference between *fiancée* and *wife*, even if it felt like a mile-wide chasm to Ryan right now. "I'm heading over to Vicki's studio now."

"Hope you don't mind if I ask, but she doesn't happen to have any sisters, does she?"

Ryan shook his head. "Sorry, man. Vicki's an only child."

But she'd get a kick out of finding out that Stuart obviously had a crush on her. Of course, Ryan couldn't blame him—at least as long as the guy always kept a polite distance. Because Vicki was *his*.

And it was long past time to make it official.

* * *

Vicki's studio was on the same oceanfront property as their main house. She'd barely moved her things into his home when Ryan had started building the art studio for her. When they were in high school, he'd loved hanging out with her in her garage while she'd worked at her pottery wheel—and he still loved it just as much. He could easily sit there with her for hours while her hands carved magic from clay.

More than once, they'd made love *Ghost*-style in the airy, light-filled space, but he was still stunned to see the way she'd transformed it since he'd left this morning. Her sculptures were nowhere to be seen. All of her equipment was gone too, most likely in the storage room just off to the side of her main work-space. But he couldn't focus on what was missing, not when the most important person in his world was standing in the middle of the empty room, wearing a deep-red dress with zippers that crisscrossed her body.

She was beyond beautiful in the dress that meant so much to both of them. She'd been wearing it the night they'd finally given in to the heat, the connection, between them. She'd worn the dress again a few times since then—usually when she wanted to drive him absolutely crazy—but something told him it held an even more special meaning for them today.

"You're here." Her eyes lit with happiness as she looked at him standing on the threshold of her studio, and her voice was breathless with unrepressed desire.

He wasn't aware of walking across the room. Only that he needed her to be in his arms and to feel her mouth beneath his. Every time he kissed her, it felt like the first time all over again, just as exciting, just as thrilling. Vicki was everything he'd ever wanted in a woman—brilliant, talented, and with curves that perfectly filled his large hands. He'd dreamed about being with her for more than half his life, and he would never take holding her in his arms—and knowing her heart was his—for granted.

"I've missed you."

"Not half as bad as I've been missing you." She slid her arms tighter around his back to pull him closer. "Thank you for the flowers."

He grinned down at her. "Every time you wear this dress my mind is blown all over again."

"I know what all these zippers do to you."

"Remind me to thank Anne for the pleasure of un-wrapping you—again." Vicki had met her designer friend when they were both competing for an art fellowship, and though Anne was extremely busy with her successful fashion career, they made sure to get together at least once a month.

"Remember how much she blushed the last time you thanked her?" Vicki smiled as she said it, but too quickly, the smile trembled on her lips, then fell away completely.

"Talk to me."

She shook her head slightly. "I asked you here to seduce you."

"Talk to me first...and then you can seduce the hell out of me."

A small smile came back then, thankfully. He easily lifted her in his arms and carried her over to the window seat that looked out over the Golden Gate Bridge and the blue waters of the San Francisco Bay. Back when they were teenagers, he used to bring Chinese takeout to her parents' garage to share with her while she worked on her latest sculpture. During the past three years, they often sat right here in her studio and ate together out of the little white boxes, even though they had a fancy dining room in the main house.

Just like always, Vicki was the perfect fit in his arms, and on his lap. She was his perfect fit every-where—not just when they were skin to skin, but with his family, with his dreams, and with his plans for the future.

"You look tired." He hated to see the smudges of exhaustion beneath her eyes. "You weren't getting enough sleep while you were in Paris, were you?"

"You know I sleep well only when we're together. I can't wait to sleep in your arms tonight."

He barely held back a curse, hating that he hadn't been able to travel to Europe with her because of the inflexible demands of the baseball season.

"This past year has been such a whirlwind," she said in a soft voice. Her fingers trailed over the buttons on his shirt, and though he wished she were looking him in the eye as she spoke, he understood that she needed a little time to center her thoughts first. "It's been thrilling to really start making my mark with my art, of course. It's just what I've always wanted. At least it should be." She finally lifted her eyes to his, and they were such a clear green that he swore he could see all the way into her soul as she said, "But I want more."

"The world is yours, sweetheart. Anything you want, all you have to do is reach for it. And I'll be there beside you to help you any way I can." He brushed back a lock of her hair from her face, but it was really just an excuse to touch her soft skin. "What do you want?"

She slid her hands up from his chest so that she was cradling his face. "You." She pressed her lips to his in a kiss so soft it was barely more than a breath. And yet it resonated through him as deeply as anything ever had. "More time with you. So much more."

"I want that too." He'd been mulling things over for a while now. Three years ago, he'd offered to retire from the Hawks so that he could be with her whenever and wherever she needed him, but Vicki had insisted she didn't need him to do that. He wasn't sure if her feelings had changed, but now *he* was the one who needed it. "I've been thinking a lot about our situation and all the hours we're spending apart."

"That's why I moved my sculptures and equipment out of the studio today. Because I want you to know—I *need* you to know—that you're more important than anything else. I finished my latest commission, and I'm not going to take on any other big projects for a while. I've gotten to live out my dream of being an artist these past few years, but now I want to really focus on my dream of being *yours*."

He had so much to say to her, but first he needed to take her mouth with his. Needed to kiss her with every ounce of passion, and love, so that she'd know how much her offer meant to him.

By the time he made himself draw back, her eyes were dark with need, her skin flushed, her breath coming fast. "I love you," he told her, his voice thick with emotion.

"I love you too."

He was amazed by her generosity, by the fact that even though she clearly thought he was taking her up on her offer, she didn't seem at all upset at the thought of putting him first. But though it meant the world to him, it was his turn now to step up to the plate and hit a game-winning ball for *her*.

"But I can't let you do that for me."

Confusion whipped across her face. "Wait...when you just kissed me, I thought that was your way of saying you agreed with my plan."

"You're the most beautiful woman in the world and you're on my lap. Not kissing you is impossible." He stroked the pad of his thumb over her lush lower lip and was rewarded by a shiver. "But you've already given up enough for me. Starting with a major museum fellowship in Italy three years ago, followed by so many other opportunities that you've said no to. Too many. It's my turn now, sweetheart. This World Series is going to be my last. I want to be with you, whether we're in San Francisco or traveling the world. And as a bonus, it will give me more time to take my foundation for bringing sports and arts back into schools to the next level. But most of all, I want to marry you and finally start the rest of our life together."

She stared at him as if she couldn't quite believe what he'd just said. "You're still in your pitching prime. The team will never let you go."

"My contract is up. Three years ago, when I said I would trade every single win to have spent the years we were apart with you, I meant it, and I still do. They could offer me all the money in the world to keep playing, but that won't change my mind. Or change my choice. *You.* I choose you, Vicki. Today. Tomorrow. Forever. I don't want to keep waiting. I want to start a family with you."

"We're already a family," she said. "We always have been."

"I know we are. But I want more—and I know you do too. Kids. Lots of them. Maybe even a dog that we know we'll actually be here to play with."

As a pitcher, Ryan was known for speed, but even though he'd asked Vicki to marry him only weeks after they'd come together again as adults, they hadn't rushed into a wedding. Not when he'd known that she still had healing to do because of the scars her first marriage had left on her heart. But he couldn't wait anymore—and he hoped she felt the same way.

He slid his hands into her hair and tangled them there as he told her, "Conflicting schedules have kept us apart for too many years. I won't let it happen again. I don't want to wait any longer. I want to get married right after the World Series is over."

Her eyes grew even bigger than when he'd told her he was going to leave the Hawks. "And here I thought I was going to surprise *you* today. You want to plan a wedding in two weeks?"

He grinned. "Actually, I was thinking about asking my mom and sisters to plan it."

"You were not." She raised an eyebrow when he didn't stop grinning. "Okay, so you clearly were, but you won't. Two weeks is going to be tough, especially with you needing to focus on the World Series, but I'll pull it off."

"Is that a yes?" he asked, desperate for that to be her answer.

She gripped his shirt in her fist and tugged him in for a kiss. God, she tasted so sweet and felt like heaven as she moved her curves closer on his lap. "Of course it's a yes. I can't wait to marry you. I've wanted to be yours since I was fifteen years old and I tackled you to the grass before that car could run you down."

She was already beginning to undo the buttons on his shirt when he made his move, flipping them over so that she was lying, beautiful, beneath him on the cushions of the window seat. "You've been mine since that moment we met. Even when we were apart. Even when we were with other people—"

She put a finger to his lips. "None of the others mattered."

He kissed her finger before gently moving it so that he could say, "They did. Because we learned something from all of them. Learned what we didn't want—and what we did."

"You," she said again as she slipped another button on his shirt free, making his heart pound hard and fast beneath her incredibly talented hands. "I want you."

He took her mouth, loving all the delicious flavors of her taste, her kisses. "You're mine. And I'm yours."

The smile she gave him was full of so much sensuality it made his head spin. He wanted her—needed her so badly—that he wasn't exactly sure how their clothes came off. Maybe she did it, maybe he did. All he knew was that they were soon skin to skin, mouth to mouth, hand to hand, with nothing between them but their beating hearts.

Holding her hands on either side of her head, he levered his hips between her thighs and looked into her beautiful eyes. "I love you."

Her fingers tightened over his as she wrapped her legs around his hips. "I love you too."

They came together in one perfect thrust, both of them losing their breath as her hips rose to meet his.

"This." He could barely speak. Could barely think or even breathe. Could only marvel that she was his. "This is how we're going to spend our honeymoon." He moved inside her and drank in the beautiful sounds of her panting at the sweet sensation of their bodies coming together. "It's going to be weeks of constantly taking each other higher." He thrust into her gorgeously slick heat again, and her eyes fluttered shut for a few moments as pleasure took her over. "Going deeper. And then deeper still." He lowered his mouth to the fluttering pulse at her neck. "And loving each other better with every single second."

"*Yes.*" She moaned the word even as she arched so that her breasts were pressed hard against him. "I can't wait to be alone and naked with you for weeks and weeks."

Just the vision of being this way with the woman he loved, heart and soul, for weeks on end made it nearly impossible to hold on much longer. "Let me watch you, Vicki. I need to feel you let go for me." He bent to lick over the taut peaks of both breasts, one after the other. "There's nothing more beautiful. Nothing I crave more than feeling you come apart in my arms."

She'd been squirming beneath his tongue on her breasts, but as he lifted his head to look into her eyes, he knew she was doing exactly as he'd asked. Letting him watch as she dropped every wall, forgot every fear, for him.

For *love.*

Angling their hips so that he was touching her core, pure pleasure and the sweetest possible joy infused her expression. "Come with me, Ryan."

"*Always.*"

Sliding his hands from hers, he wrapped them around her body and held her as closely as she was now holding him. Closer than he'd ever believed it was possible to be with another person.

Until Vicki.

He echoed every stroke, every thrust of his hips with his tongue against hers. And as they kissed and pleasure climbed, then spiked so high that the fall was inevitable—and so damned good it blew his mind all over again—something told Ryan they wouldn't be waiting until after the World Series to start their family.

Hopefully, they'd started today.

CHAPTER THREE

Sunday lunch at Mary Sullivan's house in Palo Alto was always a good—and loud—time. Especially now that there could sometimes be more than a dozen adults in the backyard, and plenty of little kids running around, as well.

Gabe and Megan's daughter Summer was the oldest at ten. Chase and Chloe's daughter Emma was the second oldest at three, followed closely by Sophie and Jake's twins, Smith and Jackie. Chase and Chloe's baby, Julia, and Gabe and Megan's son, Logan, were both talking and just starting to walk.

The family's pets were there too, of course, with Zach and Heather's dogs and Summer's poodle following Lori's cat around the yard as if they were three of her loyal subjects. All of them were great with the kids, even the little ones who didn't quite understand how rude it was to tug a tail.

Nearly everyone in the Bay Area had been able to make it today. Only Smith and Valentina were out of town, finishing up a film shoot. With a crowd like this, Mary usually kept the meal simple—hot dogs, hamburgers, grilled chicken, and salad greens picked from Lori and Grayson's farm in Pescadero. And, of course, wine from Marcus and Nicola's Napa vineyard. Sophie passed around homemade ice cream sandwiches that had Lori groaning about her dancer's figure disappearing even as she ate two in rapid succession.

For Mary, family was—and had always been—everything. She never took these Sunday lunches for granted. And even though her husband, Jack, had passed away far too many years ago when he was forty-eight, she never felt alone. Not when she could see a part of him in every single one of her kids and grandchildren.

Chase had just pulled out his camera—he'd happily been the family photographer since Jack gave him his first camera when he was eight years old—when Zach stood, tugging Heather up with him. "Listen up, everyone. Heather and I have an announcement to make."

Mary loved all her kids dearly, loved how unique they all were too. Zach had always sped through life, so it was fitting that he restored race cars and raced them for a living. When Heather had appeared in his life from out of the blue with her big, sweet Great Dane at her side, Zach had been thrown for the biggest—and best—loop of his life. It had been a joy to watch her son fall for such a wonderful woman, even if the path to true love hadn't been easy for either of them. Mary's eyes grew a little damp as she watched the two of them standing together in the sunlight, surrounded by family.

"Are you going to be making your announcement soon?" Lori asked. "Or should I go get another ice cream sandwich first?"

Lori had always been a handful. Nicknamed *Naughty*, Lori had been a whirlwind of energy even as a toddler. Her career as a dancer and choreographer suited her perfectly. As did her husband, Grayson. He seemed extra protective of her today, Mary noticed. Just as she'd noted her daughter's extreme appreciation for ice cream sandwiches. Lori had always enjoyed food, and certainly burned enough calories dancing, but three desserts was a lot even for her. As Mary looked out across the yard to where the kids were making a fort out of empty cardboard boxes, hope lit in her heart that there'd be yet another big announcement coming soon.

"Stay in your seat, Naughty," Zach said. Pausing only to grin at his fiancée, he told them all, "Heather and I are getting married in two weeks."

"Yay!"

Sophie's happy exclamation had Julia, Chase and

Chloe's baby, clapping along with her. Lori and Sophie were twins, but because Sophie was generally calmer and more soft-spoken, she had been given the nickname *Nice*.

Zach turned to Marcus. "Happen to know if your winery has an opening for a wedding on November fifteenth?"

Of course, Mary's oldest nodded. Marcus had always taken care of his younger siblings, even before Jack passed away. "Nicola and I were just talking about how it's been too long since one of you got married at the vineyard."

"Great, then it's settled." Zach looked extremely pleased as he turned to give Heather a quick, and very possessive, kiss. "See you all in Napa on the fifteenth."

"Actually—" Ryan surprised them all by standing up, bringing Vicki with him. "We have an announcement too."

"Ryan." Vicki put one hand on his face to turn his gaze to hers. "We can wait."

"No. We can't. We won't."

Mary was struck by how fierce her normally easy-going son looked. Everything in life had always come easily to him—especially baseball. Only love had been a struggle when he'd fallen head over heels for Vicki as a teenager, then lost her when she moved away and married another man. Vicki had always been, and would always be, her son's forever love.

Vicki turned to everyone at the table. "I'm sure you've all guessed this by now, but we were planning to tell you about our wedding plans too."

"For the fifteenth," Ryan said, looking straight at Zach.

"You've got to be kidding me." Lori looked between her brothers. "You've both decided to get married on the same day? A day that's only *two weeks* away?" She shook her head. "I'm really glad I didn't go get that ice cream sandwich after all."

Just like similar times when Lori had razzed them when they were kids, Zach and Ryan both looked on the verge of snarling—or worse—at their sister.

"We can change our date," Heather offered.

But Zach wasn't having any of it. "Two weeks, Heather, or it's a guy dressed like Elvis at Vegas's finest by-the-hour chapel."

Mary could barely smother her grin. Especially when Summer ran up to the table and said, "What's going on?" She picked up baby Logan from Gabe's lap and bounced her little brother in her arms, making him laugh with delight. "Why are Uncle Zach and Uncle Ryan standing there looking so mad at each other?"

Gabe didn't bother to contain his own laughter as he told his stepdaughter, "Because they're not seeing the obvious answer, even though it's right in front of them." Though Gabe fought fires for a living, Mary had always thought his solid, steady personality would have made him a great mediator. It certainly made him a great husband to Megan and father to their two kids.

Chase looked at his brother, grinning as he nodded. "Makes perfect sense to me."

"Couldn't agree more," Marcus said. "Smith and Valentina are definitely going to be bummed they missed this lunch."

"What the hell are you all talking about?" Both Zach and Ryan erupted at the same time.

Sophie's eyes were sparkling as she told her brothers in a gentle, but clearly amused voice, "We all think you should have a double wedding."

Zach and Ryan looked at their wives-to-be first, then each other. Barely a year apart in age, they'd always been extra close, whether they were running around together or arguing about something that made sense only to the two of them.

Mary didn't want to sway them, but she couldn't deny her gut feeling that a double wedding would be absolutely perfect for them. "Why don't the four of you go talk through this idea?" she suggested.

As Zach, Heather, Ryan, and Vicki headed toward the garage—the place where plenty of things had been hashed out between the siblings over the years—Mary shot Lori an affectionate warning glance to make it clear that she should not follow her brothers or their fiancées out of the backyard to lend her opinion on how they should proceed with their wedding plans.

"What if they need a referee?" Lori asked around the new ice cream sandwich she'd somehow managed to get hold of without ever leaving the table. Mary grinned as she saw little Emma crawl out from beneath the table, her mouth sticky with the bite of dessert she'd taken before handing it off to her Aunt Lori.

Chase, Marcus, and Gabe all looked at each other to see who was going to volunteer to step between the two brothers if things went south during their discussion in the garage. But it was Sophie who stood up.

"I'll go." She leaned down to kiss her husband, Jake. "Wish me luck."

Everyone had thought Sophie and Jake were such a strange match at first, the quiet librarian and the tattooed pub owner. But Mary had always known they were meant for each other. What could she say? It was a mother's intuition. Watching them together now—and seeing what great parents they were to their twins—made her so happy. And reminded her of her own true love.

Looking up at the clouds in the blue sky above, she swore they formed a smile. "Grandma, look!" Summer put an arm around her and pointed up at the sky. "The clouds are smiling at us."

"They are, aren't they?" Mary brought her grand-daughter closer and held her tight.

* * *

"Pick a different date," Zach ordered his brother.

"Nope." Ryan held firm. "We're all set on the fif-teenth, thanks."

Zach and Ryan were nose to nose when Sophie stepped into the garage. Heather and Vicki were two very strong women—they had to be to live with and love über-alpha men like Sophie's brothers. But clearly, even the two of them were wary about getting be-tween the brothers at present.

Deciding to let her brothers keep up their chest beating for the time being, Sophie headed for the women who were already sisters to her, even if no official vows had been made yet.

"What do you want to do?" She figured there was no point in being anything but direct at this point. "Does a double wedding sound like something that could work? Or do you each want your own separate wedding?" Before either of them could answer, she added, "And don't think we won't understand if separate weddings are your choice. You know how we can get carried away with an idea, especially when we're all together like this."

"Actually," Heather spoke first, "the more I think

about it, the more I like the idea of a double wedding. Especially with you, Vicki. Right from the first time we met, I liked you. And over the past few years, you've become one of my closest friends."

"I feel the exact same way." Vicki grinned. "Let's do it. Let's pull a Sullivan first with a double wedding."

"Boys," Sophie called out. "It's all decided." She smiled as Zach and Ryan turned to face the women. "You're having a double wedding. And it's going to be awesome."

Zach was at Heather's side so fast it was as if he'd become one of his race cars. "Heather, we don't have to do this just because—"

"I want to." Heather put her hands on either side of Zach's face, and Sophie's heart melted at how much love she saw in her brother's eyes when he looked at his fiancée.

Heather had utterly transformed Zach in all the best possible ways. So had the dogs, who must have realized that Zach and Heather had left the backyard and were now barreling in through the garage door to find them.

"All this time that we've been waiting to pick the date, maybe this was why," Heather said. "Because we were supposed to do this with family—" She smiled at Ryan. "—and friends." She turned her smile to Vicki.

Zach didn't speak for a long moment, just searched

Heather's eyes as though he wanted to make absolutely sure that she wasn't just trying to make his family happy with a double wedding. Only once the dogs had wiggled between them did he finally crack a smile. "If it's what you want."

"Don't you?" She turned to where Ryan and Vicki were standing, holding hands. "I know you're close to your whole family. But the two of you—"

"You've always been closest to each other," Vicki cut in. She turned to Ryan. "I can see it already, how if you multiply what we feel for each other with what Heather and Zach feel—" Her smile was radiant. "—it's going to be like all the love in the world is right there in Marcus's vineyard on the fifteenth."

Sophie could see that Ryan didn't need any more convincing. Not when Vicki's smile told him everything he needed to know. "If you're in, so am I." He kissed her before turning back to Zach. "You good with this?"

Zach looked at Heather one more time, looking for her smile, before he turned back to Ryan and nodded. "I'm good."

Sophie breathed a silent sigh of relief as her brothers shook hands. Then she looped one arm through Heather's and one through Vicki's. "Now, if you'll excuse us, we have some double-wedding planning to do."

CHAPTER FOUR

The following day, more than half a dozen Sullivan women gathered together in Chase and Chloe's living room. Those who couldn't be there in person dialed in via Skype. The coffee table was laden with cheese, crackers, grapes, and Megan's very organized lists of what needed to be done—and who was going to do it.

Heather had been running Top Dog, her dog-training and day care center in San Francisco, for almost a decade, and yet she was still boggled by the seemingly endless details of putting together a big family wedding with only two weeks' notice. Granted, she'd never been all that focused on traditionally female things, like clothes or shoes or weddings. Sometimes it still made her laugh to think that she'd ended up with a man who knew more about those things than she did. Not that Zach wasn't all man, of course. Just thinking of the decidedly alpha way he'd woken her up this morning had her shivering at the delicious memories.

He wasn't only naughty—he was completely incorrigible. And she loved every single second of it.

There was no other man she'd ever let strip all of her defenses away. Only Zach.

"Thank God for you and your spreadsheets, Megan." Heather smiled across the coffee table at her soon-to-be sister-in-law to reinforce her gratitude.

"You've already put so much time into working on the wedding," Vicki agreed. Judging by the smears of white clay on her cheeks, hair, and hands, Heather guessed Vicki had come straight to the meeting from her studio. "We know you're busy with two kids and your CPA business, so if you want us to take it from here—"

"Are you kidding?" Megan grinned. "I *love* spreadsheets. And using them to plan your double wedding is pretty much the most fun thing ever. Gabe was actually teasing me about it last night." Heather found the flush in Megan's cheeks when she brought up her firefighter husband totally adorable. They were the sweetest family with ten-year-old Summer and baby Logan.

"I love spreadsheets too," Kerry Dromoland said over the computer screen. She was not only one of the finest wedding planners in the Pacific Northwest, she'd also recently gotten engaged to Zach's cousin Adam, who was an architect specializing in historic renovations in Seattle. "I'm sorry I can't do more to help, especially when putting on weddings is what I do for a living."

"Please don't apologize for anything, Kerry," Vicki said. "You're already juggling four weddings that you've been hired to put on in the next two weeks, so you should be giving them your full attention. And the master checklists you sent us have been super helpful."

Heather looked at the women gathered together in Chase and Chloe's living room, the most central meeting location for the group. Lori had come north from her farm in Pescadero and Nicola south from her vineyard in Napa. "We're so grateful to all of you."

"All four of us are grateful," Vicki agreed. "Even if Ryan has to be at the stadium to get ready for the first World Series game—"

"And Zach would rather have a root canal than be on a wedding-planning committee." Lori's statement had everyone laughing at the truth of it.

"Chloe and Lori," Vicki continued, "you're saving our butts big-time by putting together the look of the wedding and choreographing where everyone needs to be during the double ceremony. And Sophie, we are hugely thankful for your encyclopedic knowledge of the Sullivan family tree and all its various branches all over the world. I know you offered to call and email everyone in addition to sending the invitations, but—"

"It's my pleasure," Sophie assured them. "It's been too long since I've spoken to some of our relatives anyway." She looked down at the long list of names. "How did I not know that Jansen is now living in Prague?"

Zach and Ryan's mother, Mary, leaned over to explain, "Jansen is one of their second cousins once removed on Jack's side."

Heather couldn't keep from laughing out loud. Yes, this double wedding was a daunting task, but it was already so much fun getting to spend time working on it with so many amazing women. She'd never dreamed of having such a big family, but boy, did she enjoy every second of it. Falling in love with a Sullivan meant falling for all of them. And she couldn't *wait* to make it official.

Back when she'd first met Zach, she'd been certain he was a player. After all, with his perfectly chiseled face, blue eyes, broad shoulders, and effortless charm, how could he be anything else?

But she'd been wrong. Totally wrong. Zach Sullivan loved with everything in him. His family. The dogs.

And especially *her*.

Heather's dog, Atlas, had seen Zach's true character from the start. Heather had saved her Great Dane from a dangerous and neglectful puppy mill, so he had never been very comfortable around men. But he'd been Zach's biggest fan from day one.

Turning to Nicola, she added more thanks. "It means so much to us that you've offered to sing at the wedding."

"Actually, I have some really fun news about that." Heather had spent so much time with Nicola over the past few years that it was hard to remember she was one of the biggest pop stars in the world. She was married to Zach's oldest brother, Marcus, and when Nicola wasn't touring to support her music, they lived on an extraordinary vineyard property in Napa Valley. "Mia's husband, Ford, and our mutual friend Drew Morrison would both like to play at your wedding with me, if that's okay with you."

Heather turned to Vicki in shock. Her friend's expression mirrored her own. "Are you really asking if it's *okay* with us?" She knew she probably looked like a fool right now, but this wedding was already so far beyond her wildest dreams, she felt as if she could barely get her brain to fire correctly anymore. "That would be *incredible.*"

"Beyond incredible," Vicki echoed.

"Ford can't wait." Mia beamed at them through the computer monitor from her desk in Seattle. "He was just saying how it's been too long since we all got together. And what better reason than a wedding? I so wish I could be there in person with all of you. It sure looks more fun than the showing I have in fifteen minutes with the most uptight couple you've ever met in your life." She made a face. "But before I go, I wanted to give you even more good news. I convinced the property managers at those two estates next to Marcus and Nicola's winery to let us have the houses for the wedding weekend."

"That's great news, Mia. Thank you." Heather knew that Zach's cousin Mia was the top Realtor in Seattle, but the Napa Valley estates weren't even vacation rentals. They were private homes. How on earth had Mia managed to persuade the owners to let them use them?

As if she could read Heather's mind, Sophie said, "Mia always has had a magic touch."

"All Sullivan women do." Lori winked at the group. "Speaking of magic, I was just on the phone with Brooke during my drive into the city. She's really sorry she couldn't make this meeting, but she said she's pushing off her retail orders for the next two weeks so that she can focus on making special chocolates for your wedding."

Heather wasn't much of a crier—and she knew Vicki wasn't either—but both of them got a little sniffly at that point.

Heather and Zach had agreed to wait until after the

wedding to tell his family their big news, but she simply couldn't hold it in anymore. Not when she was surrounded by such love. And not when she knew for sure that her children were never going to grow up the way she had—with parents whose lies had made her question whether real love actually existed. Now she knew for sure that love was real. Zach and his family proved it to her every single day.

"I have news too."

Zach would take a bullet for anyone in his family—and so would Heather. She looked around the room at the women who had become her best friends in the world. Her sisters in every way that counted. Finally, she got to Mary. Zach's mother was one of the warmest people on the planet, and from the overjoyed look in her eyes, Heather knew she had already guessed her news.

"Zach and I are going to have a baby." Heather's hand automatically went to her still-flat stomach.

Every woman in the room leaped to her feet for what amounted to the best group hug *ever*.

"I'm so happy for you." Vicki held on to Heather even after the other women had moved away to open up a bottle of wine and toast each other. "No wonder Zach was so insistent about keeping the wedding date no matter what. Ryan and I can move ours so that the fifteenth can be all yours."

"No way." By now, Heather couldn't imagine having any other wedding. "Ryan also looked really intense about making sure he married you in two weeks. And I know it's what you want, as well."

Vicki hugged Heather again. "Promise me you'll save a spot on your mantel. Because I just got the perfect idea for your wedding gift."

Heather and Zach were already lucky enough to own one of Vicki's sculptures. Though they now sold in the mid-six figures, last Christmas Vicki had given them clay figurines of Atlas and Cuddles curled up together in the dog bed they shared. It was one of Heather's most prized possessions and made her smile every time she looked at it.

"I've got a good idea for you too," Heather said. One of her favorite dogs that came to Top Dog—a miniature poodle and Pekingese mix—was about to have a litter of puppies. By the time the puppies were nine weeks old and ready to find homes, Ryan and Vicki should be back from their honeymoon. If they wanted one of the sweet little bundles of fur, she'd make sure they could have first pick.

Heather and Vicki had only just sat down when little Emma, Jackie, and Smith came barreling out of Chloe's back room where her babysitter was watching the kids during the wedding planning. The college student had baby Logan on one arm and baby Julia on the other as she chased the bigger kids. "Sorry, they heard everyone cheering and were desperate to be a part of the celebrations."

"Mommy!" Emma climbed into Chloe's outstretched arms. "What did we miss?"

Chloe nuzzled her daughter before looking at Heather. When she nodded, Chloe said, "Aunt Heather and Uncle Zach are going to have a baby."

With unerring aim, Emma threw herself into Heather's arms and gave her a big wet kiss on the lips. "I love more babies!"

"We do too," Smith and Jackie agreed as they got on Heather's lap too.

Though Sophie told her twins to be careful that they weren't crushing Heather, she felt anything but. Wrapping her arms around the three kids as best she could, Heather closed her eyes and let herself savor all the happiness she'd once been so afraid she could never have.

CHAPTER FIVE

Vicki could sit in the stands for a thousand World Series games, and she'd never get used to the butterflies in her stomach. Every time Ryan let a ball rip, she held her breath. And every time he struck out yet another batter, she nearly lost her voice from screaming his name. The Hawks were behind 3–4 at the top of the seventh inning, and the series was tied at one game apiece. If this was to be Ryan's final season, she wanted him to go out on a high.

Fortunately, though, Ryan didn't look nervous at all. She was always amazed by how calmly he approached his job. He'd been like that even as a teenager—so steady and confident without being cocky. *Fun first, winning second* was his motto.

She'd learned so much from him, not only how to be more steady and confident, but also how to love with her whole heart. And how to trust that she would be loved back.

After striking out the third batter in a row, Ryan

blew her a kiss from the mound. She blew him one back as the butterflies danced in her stomach for an entirely different reason now. He laughed as he reached out with his mitt to "catch" her kiss, and she was struck for the millionth time how wonderful it was to be with someone who was always laughing, always filled with such joy.

Every time they made love, she felt utterly cherished, but last night had been extra special. Almost as if the knowledge that they were close to finally making their vows to each other had amped up their emotions. Of course, it didn't hurt that for all his laid-back ease, Ryan was alpha to the core when it came to lovemaking.

Three years ago, just after their fake engagement had been announced, another woman had asked Vicki how it felt to tame the ultimate bad boy. She'd replied that he was nowhere close to being tame, and truer words had never been spoken. Because after the deliciously wicked things he'd done to her last night— things that made her feel owned, possessed, and claimed in all the best possible ways—she could confidently say that Ryan Sullivan would never be anywhere close to *tame*.

"You two are still so adorable together," Ryan's sister Lori commented as she found her seat when the seventh-inning stretch began. "I always think how sweet it is that you've been in love with each other since high school." Lori and her husband, Grayson, had been caught in bad traffic and had just arrived holding a huge tub of popcorn for everyone to munch from. Lori obviously hadn't waited to start snacking, as her question came around a mouthful of kernels. "Any crazy new wedding requests come in since last night?"

Vicki laughed. "Not yet."

Lori looked down at Ryan's team in their dugout. "Ballplayers can be so weird. Weird but hot. Although nowhere near as hot as my cowboy." She looked up to where Grayson was walking down the stands, his arms full of boxes of candy. "Look at how all the girls in the stands are shamelessly drooling over him. I'm going to have to make it clear that he's all mine."

Vicki couldn't stifle her grin as Grayson came into their box and Lori planted a majorly hot kiss on him in front of the whole world. Somehow he managed to keep one hand on the candy while taking a handful of his wife in the other. By the time they pulled back, everyone in the stands was watching, wide-eyed.

Everyone except Zach and Heather, who had eyes only for each other a couple of seats away. Vicki wasn't at all surprised to see how protective he was of his pregnant fiancée. Zach had always been the biggest player of the bunch, but Vicki now knew it was true what they said about reformed rakes: They really did make the best mates. Zach was utterly devoted to the woman he loved. Just the way *all* Sullivans were devoted to their significant others.

More than once, Vicki had been tempted to pinch herself to make sure this was really her life. She was an army brat who'd moved more than she stayed. She never got to have a close circle of friends until the Sullivans had taken her in when she was fifteen and made her feel like she finally belonged. Even then, she'd made some huge missteps, especially marrying the wrong man and staying with him for ten too-long years. Every single day of the past three years, she had been amazed by the love she'd managed to find—the love she'd rediscovered—with Ryan.

Their love made any amount of hard work to put on this double wedding absolutely worth it. They'd all been working pedal to the metal on it for the past week and, amazingly, it had been mostly smooth sailing. A majority of the guests were able to clear their schedules, even on such short notice. And Vicki was pretty sure that neither she nor Heather had been particularly high maintenance.

When it came to their men, on the other hand?

She and Heather had to laugh at just how similar Ryan's and Zach's professions were—especially all the superstitions that preceded each of Ryan's games and Zach's races.

Ryan himself wasn't particularly superstitious, thankfully. But his teammates were, which was why the Hawks insisted that Ryan and Vicki walk through an arch of baseball bats to get to the altar. Okay, so it might not be the most romantic vision in the world, but Vicki was willing to roll with it. Thank God he didn't believe in staying celibate during the series, like so many of his teammates. After having been away in France for two weeks, even the mere *thought* of another two weeks in which they couldn't make love would have pushed both of them over the edge.

Surprisingly, Zach's racing colleagues were even nuttier about the wedding than Ryan's baseball team. First, Zach's pit crew claimed that if anything green was used in any part of the decorations (apart from the grass and grapevines, which obviously couldn't be changed), Zach would lose all future races. But they were even more serious about Zach not shaving off so much as a millimeter of his facial hair between now and the wedding. To do so, they insisted, would be the ultimate jinx.

"Since we've got a few minutes before the game starts again and three out of four of you are here," Lori's twin, Sophie, said, "I thought we could get some extra wedding business done."

"Megan isn't here," Lori groaned, "and we can't do anything without her spreadsheets, right?"

"Got them right here." Sophie lifted her tablet. "We decided to put the spreadsheets in the cloud so that we can all access them, remember?"

"You sound like our cousin Suzanne when you start talking about computer clouds," Lori grumbled.

Suzanne was the only female sibling of the four New York Sullivans—Drake, Harrison, and Alec were her brothers. Vicki had spent some time with each of them over the years while on trips to New York and at weddings, of course. Now that she and Ryan were going to have more free time, she hoped she could get to know his cousins in New York and Maine better. Thankfully, she was already really close with the Seattle crew—Rafe, Mia, Ian, Dylan, Adam, and their parents, Claudia and Max.

"Speaking of our cousins in New York," Sophie said, "Alec has made arrangements to use a few of his private planes to fly family from New York and Maine into a private airstrip in Napa."

None of the Sullivans flaunted their money or fame, but since Vicki hadn't grown up knowing people who had private planes or who were famous, stuff like this still made her head spin.

"And Heather," Sophie continued, "Alec wanted you to know that he'd be happy to pick up your parents in Washington, DC, if that would be more convenient for them."

Heather did her best to try to hide her reaction from the rest of them, but Vicki knew too much about Heather's fractured relationship with her parents to miss it as she said, "I'll give them a call and let Alec know right away if they'd like a ride."

Judging by the way Zach pulled Heather closer, it was obvious that he wasn't particularly thrilled about Heather's parents coming to the wedding. Vicki wished she could do something to help, but sometimes the very best you could do was simply to be there for the people you loved. Ryan and his family had shown this to Vicki time and again.

Lori shoved the rest of the chocolate bar she'd been eating into her mouth before saying, "Are we still going to go see your wedding gowns after the game?"

Vicki had always known that she wanted Anne to make her wedding dress. Fortunately, while her friend had catapulted straight to the top of the fashion world, she'd still offered to squeeze in two last-second dresses for Vicki and Heather.

"I'm really looking forward to seeing Anne again," Vicki said. "She's been so busy flying around the world opening her new boutiques in Paris and Rome that it's been months since we've really had a chance to chat."

"I'm dying to see what she's got planned for both of you," Sophie said. "I've got a borderline unhealthy fixation on her dresses."

"You're not the only one," Vicki said.

Ryan had a bit of a fixation, as well, given that the first time they'd made love she'd been wearing one of Anne's dresses—the sexy red one she'd worn in the studio just the other day. It had been the night of their fake engagement party, and she still remembered the way it had felt when she and Ryan finally gave in to their feelings for each other and he stripped her dress away, one zipper at a time.

Heather and Anne had met only once, via Skype, but Anne had taken one look at Zach's fiancée and declared that she knew exactly the dress she should wear. Anne might change her technicolor hair weekly and have a good dozen piercings—but she was a master when it came to knowing exactly how to bring out the best in a woman. Even things the woman wearing the dress might not be able to see in herself.

When the players ran out onto the field, Sophie shelved wedding planning so that they could watch the rest of the game. One that turned out to be a total nail-biter by the ninth inning, with the score at 5–4 and the Hawks in the lead, thankfully.

Ryan was back up at the mound, and though he still didn't look nervous, Vicki could see just how fierce his concentration was. The only other time he ever looked that focused was when they were in bed and he was utterly intent on her pleasure. One after the other, he struck the first two batters out, his fastballs precise and explosive.

Soon after, the third batter, already down two strikes, stepped back up to the plate. Lori gripped one of Vicki's hands, and Sophie took the other.

"You can do it, Ryan." Sophie's whispered words echoed those in Vicki's head.

Vicki figured the batter was assuming another fastball would be coming his way. But she knew how foolish it was to think that Ryan's easy demeanor meant he wasn't working out how to get exactly what he wanted. Three years ago, he'd wanted *her*. And boy, had he ever gone out of his way to make sure that happened...

Another delicious shiver was moving through her at the memories of the first time they'd kissed—and then had made the sweetest love possible—when Ryan turned his head just enough to catch her eye. She smiled and mouthed, *I love you,* and the next thing she knew, the perfect curve ball was flying from his fingers.

A curve ball the batter never saw coming.

The entire stadium leaped to its feet as Ryan's team rushed to the mound to lift him up on their shoulders. The second he was set down on the ground, he headed straight for Vicki. She was already more than halfway to him by the time he leaped over the fence and swung her up into his arms. The moment he crushed his mouth to hers, the crowd's cheers easily jumped a full decibel.

But all Vicki heard in his kiss—all she felt, all she knew—was how much Ryan loved her.

More than enough to fill this stadium a million times over.

CHAPTER SIX

Since Smith and Valentina had missed out on the wedding planning due to their filming schedule in Denmark, they insisted on throwing the combined bachelorette and bachelor party the night before the wedding. And with the Hawks having just won the World Series—again—there was also plenty of bubbly flowing to toast Ryan's retirement from baseball at the very top of his game.

As Marcus and Nicola's Napa Valley home was currently being decorated for the wedding, Smith and Valentina had booked Castello di Amorosa for the party. Children and adults alike were all having a marvelous time exploring the vineyard estate that was built to be a near-perfect replica of a thirteenth-century Tuscan castle.

Once upon a time, Zach Sullivan hadn't just believed he'd never marry—he'd never expected to fall in love either. For a man who hated to be proved wrong, nothing could have made him happier than knowing just how off base he'd been about love and marriage.

Tonight, Heather was stunning him, yet again, in a sky-blue dress that skimmed over her curves while highlighting her long legs. He couldn't keep his hands to himself. Thankfully, his bride didn't mind in the least—especially given that she wasn't doing much better at keeping her hands off him.

Little Emma had just given her a bunch of flowers, and Heather was smelling them with a happy smile on her lips—one that fell the moment she realized her parents had arrived at the party.

A muscle jumped in Zach's jaw as he watched her put down the flowers to go say hello. The Linseys put on a good show of being a happy couple, but that was all it was: a performance.

Zach's family had promised him they would step in with her parents any way they could. As good as their word, Smith and Valentina wasted no time coming over.

"Mr. and Mrs. Linsey, it's great to finally meet you." Smith had on his best movie-star smile, one that looked genuine even if his heart wasn't truly behind it. "If we could steal you away from your daughter for a short while, Valentina and I would love to give you both a tour of the castle."

Simply getting to meet a movie star like Smith would be more than enough for most people, so Zach figured there was no way they would turn down the chance to spend one-on-one time with Smith and his fiancée.

"Honey," Heather's father said, "you don't mind if your mother and I step away for a few minutes while you celebrate with your friends?"

"No, you should absolutely go!"

Heather seemed to realize a moment too late just how enthusiastic she sounded, but Zach was already stepping into the fray. "Heather and I actually have a few things we need to discuss for tomorrow." He forced himself to smile at her parents, though he suspected it looked more like he was baring his teeth. "Enjoy your tour with Smith and Valentina."

After the four of them had walked around the corner, and Zach took Heather in the opposite direction, she asked, "We don't really have anything to discuss for the wedding, do we?"

Zach stopped to give her a kiss before saying, "We do, but not here."

Earlier, he'd made a mental note about a stone cottage on the property that would be perfect for a little alone time with his fiancée. A few minutes later, when they were inside the small building, he drew Heather into his arms.

He stroked her back to loosen the tight muscles, and she breathed out a small sigh of relaxation. "I owe

Smith and Valentina big time for this. I've always loved your family, but I love them even more now for going out of their way to keep my parents occupied."

"They're happy to help," he told her. "Everyone is."

Zach had always been more in tune with Heather than anyone else—so even without her saying more, he knew she was not only overwhelmed by her parents being here, but also that her first trimester was tiring her out more than she wanted to admit.

"It's not too late, you know," he said as he pulled her down to sit with him on a plush couch, slipping off her heels so that he could rub her feet. "We could hop a plane to Vegas tonight and skip the rest of the wedding craziness."

"I could never do that when everyone has done so much and worked so hard to make our day perfect." She looked up into his eyes, and his heart squeezed as she said, "It's just that when my parents walked in, and I realized just how big a contrast your family makes to mine. I guess it's just a little hard to swallow tonight."

Zach wanted to soothe her, wanted to tell her everything would be okay, wanted to do whatever he could to steal away her pain. But he knew she was still thinking, still trying to put her feelings into words, so he forced himself to remain quiet.

Her voice was soft when she spoke again. "Even

your two-hundred-mile-an-hour races hardly scare me
that much anymore, because I know how much
control you have over the vehicle. And I stopped
measuring you against my father practically right from
the start, because you're nothing like him. Nothing at
all." She sighed. "So why does the idea of getting
married still sort of freak me out?"

Zach moved his hands from her feet to slowly run
them down her arms, over the crisscrossing of scars.
She'd started cutting herself as a teenager after she
found out the father she'd always adored had been
cheating on her mother for their entire marriage.
Heather was strong, confident, and sassy—yet Zach
knew she still felt phantom pain sometimes when she
had to deal with her father.

"Some scars run deep. So deep that even when we
think they're healed, they might not be. Not completely." Zach held her gaze as he prepared to admit to his
own scars that were still healing. "I can't help but think
about my dad tonight. I've been thinking about him
more and more since we got engaged. Since I found
out I'm going to be a father myself."

She lifted her hand to his cheek, which was covered
with the hair his superstitious race crew insisted he
keep from shaving off. Fortunately, Heather seemed to
like it when he got scruffy. "Do you still worry that
you're going to follow in his footsteps?"

His father, Jack, died of an aneurysm when Zach was seven. Out of all eight kids, Zach was the one who looked the most, and acted the most, like his father, so he'd grown up believing that he wouldn't see past forty-eight either. This was why Zach had never planned to fall in love—because he hadn't thought he could count on tomorrow. It was also why he'd gone for speed his whole life, to experience as much as he could before it was over.

But then he'd met Heather. And everything he'd once believed to be true had been flipped upside down and inside out. In all the best possible ways.

Which was why he couldn't lie to her tonight, and would never want to even if he could. For thirty years he'd held his pain and fear over losing his father inside. Held it inside until Heather had made him feel safe— and loved—enough to confess it all.

"Sometimes I do still worry," he admitted. "Especially around the anniversary of his passing—or when we have big family events. Which," he added with a small smile, "seem like they happen twice a month depending on the birthday-baby-wedding schedule for the year."

"Three years ago," Heather said, "those worries were why you tried to hold back from me. So if you're still scared sometimes, how do you keep yourself from holding back now? Because I never feel that you are.

Even when you're telling me that your scars haven't gone away completely, you're not at all scared about promising me forever tomorrow, are you?"

"Falling in love with you—that was the biggest thing that made the worries fade at first." He pulled her on to his lap. "I couldn't imagine a world in which I'd ever be able to give you up. Even if I knew for sure that I wasn't going to make it past the next five years, I realized I'd still be the selfish bastard who had to have you." He kissed her for emphasis...and also because he couldn't resist the pull of her sweet mouth. "And ever since then, knowing I'm not indestructible or bullet-proof has been a good reminder to live every single day to the fullest. With you."

"I love you." She lowered her head to his shoulder. "I'm sorry I'm being weird tonight."

"You're not being weird. You're being honest, and I love you even more because you're not afraid to tell me what you're feeling. Fortunately, I happened to prepare a few bad dog jokes in case we needed them. Want to hear them?"

She lifted her head to look at him, and he was glad to see her mouth quirk up on the side. "I know you'll be bursting to tell them to me all night if you don't get them out now."

"What do you call it when a cat wins a dog show?"

"Honestly, I'm scared to even guess."

He grinned. "A cat-has-trophy."

She shook her head. "That's just awful."

"I try." He gave her another quick kiss. "What kind of dog does Dracula have?"

She leaned back into him and mumbled the answer against his neck.

"Did you just say bloodhound?" He stroked his hand down her back as she nodded. "You've been secretly reading my joke book, haven't you?"

"No," she said with a fervent shake of her head. "I swear I haven't."

He laughed and pulled her closer. "Only one more, and then you're off the hook. At least until tomorrow."

She burrowed tighter into the circle of his arms. "Go ahead. I think I'm ready now."

"I don't know if anyone could ever be ready for this one," he warned her. "What does the dog magician say when he does his tricks?" He paused a beat for maximum impact. "Labracadabra."

Though Heather couldn't help but laugh—okay, maybe it was closer to a groan—Zach knew she was still upset. Which meant it was time to move to distraction technique number two.

"Remember how I made you forget about everything, way back when?"

"How could I ever forget that squirmy, hot night sitting in a restaurant with you teasing me until I thought I was going to lose my mind?" She tightened her arms around him even as she added, "But we're at our bachelor and bachelorette party with your whole family here, and—"

He cut off her faint protests with a kiss. "All the better. If we're caught tonight, we'll be a thing of Sullivan legend." He nipped at her lip and let the kinky thought sear into her mind, even though he would never let that happen in a million years.

The first time they'd made love, she'd teased him about his *legendary* bedroom, and he'd never let her forget it. Now, as she laughed and pulled his head down for another kiss, he was glad to know that his plans to make her forget about her parents were finally working.

Heather was the first—the only—woman Zach had ever lost control with. And the truth was that he still lost it every time they were together. Lost it so completely that he soon had her dress up around her waist, his pants unzipped, and then he was inside her.

He closed his eyes and held her tight as they drove each other higher and higher. No teasing tonight. No going slow. Just the two of them reminding each other in the most elemental of ways how deep their love ran.

As she began to come apart over him, he captured her gasp of pleasure with a kiss that barely masked his own groan. For a long while, they simply held on to each other.

When he knew that someone actually might start looking for them soon, Zach gently lifted her from his lap so that they could both set their clothes to rights.

"Do I look okay?" Heather asked.

"You've never been more beautiful." He smoothed her dress down over her hips, then rested his hand over her stomach. He couldn't wait to be a father and have a little boy or girl with Heather's flashing eyes and quick wit.

"Just remember," he told her, "whatever happens, I've always got your back."

She breathed deeply, as if to inhale into her very marrow the same vow he'd made her years ago when they'd first had to get through a night with her parents. "I know. We've got this." She slid her hand into his. "Together."

* * *

Ryan had always liked Vicki's parents. She had a great relationship with them, and he was glad that her mother, father, and two brothers had all been able to come to Napa for the wedding on such short notice.

Her family had spent plenty of time in California during the past few years, but they were still clearly bowled over by the star power in the Sullivan family and circle of friends. Especially for Vicki's brothers, who were both huge baseball fans, getting to meet the Hawks at the party seemed to be a pretty big deal.

Fortunately, Ryan knew Vicki's family could take care of themselves. It was his fiancée he was most concerned about tonight. Because although she clearly loved getting to spend time with her family, Ryan could tell that something wasn't quite right. She was quieter than usual. A little less bright.

At the first chance, he took her hand and drew her away from the crowd. "Let's go for a walk." She didn't say anything as he led them out of the castle and into the vineyard that surrounded it. He took off his jacket and draped it over her shoulders to ward off the slight chill as he brought her farther up the path so that they could only faintly hear the laughter, the music.

The moon was full, and the vines were lit up as if by a romantic spotlight. When they reached a small, walled rose garden with a seat at the center, he pulled her into his arms and tipped up her chin so that he could look into her eyes. "Are you okay?"

"We're getting married tomorrow." She smiled at him, but it didn't quite reach her eyes. "How could I not be okay?"

"Vicki." He stroked her cheek. "You can tell me if you're not."

"You said the same thing to me the night your team threw us a party for our pretend engagement."

"Our love was always real," he said first. And then, "I meant it then and I mean it now—you can tell me anything. Anything at all."

She was silent for a few moments before finally saying, "After my divorce, I didn't just vow to protect my heart at all costs—I also believed I'd never marry again. But then there you were, my best friend, the one man I had never been able to stop loving. Your love made it possible for me to push my fears aside and put my entire heart and soul on the line for you. But tonight..." She paused, scrunching up her face, the same expression she got when the clay wasn't turning into the sculpture she could see in her mind's eye. "I just want the past to stay in the past. I didn't even realize any darkness from those years without you was still lingering, but tonight it feels like the final bits of my bad first marriage are being dredged up to the surface."

"I hate that we were apart all those years, Vicki." Just as he hated the pain he could see on her face right now. "I've wished a million times that I could go back into the past to redo it all. I wouldn't just fumble my way through a kiss with you at fifteen—I'd find the guts to tell you straight up that I was in love with you. I wouldn't let you marry some other guy. And I sure as hell wouldn't almost lose touch with you for fifteen years when what I most wanted was to see you, talk to you, kiss you every single day."

"I can't believe I used to think I was made for long term and you weren't," she said in a soft voice, "when I'm the one who's still scared that my earlier failure at marriage might taint the one that truly matters. I already gave my ex ten years—I don't want to give him even one more second."

"We'll never be able to erase the past," Ryan said, "but we don't need to. Because we've got tonight. Tomorrow. And every single day after that. Forever," he said as he held her hands in his. "That's how long I've loved you—and how long I always will."

"That first day, when I was so scared, you did the same thing you're doing now. You took me out into nature and held my hand and showed me that you'd be there for me, no matter what."

"You let me hold your hand that day three years ago, but I wanted to do so much more."

"Tell me, Ryan. What would you have done then, if you could have?"

"This." He pulled her even closer and kissed her. "And this." He cupped her face in his hands and stared into her eyes. "I would have said, *I love you.* I would have said, *I've always loved you and I always will.*" He brushed away her tears. "And I would have asked you not just to trust me, but to trust yourself too. All those years away from you—and then trying to pretend I didn't want you with every fiber of my being—were the worst kind of torture. But we've always come away stronger. Better. And even more in love. Which is how I know we'll make it through anything else that comes our way. Just as long as we're always honest about what we're feeling, what we need."

"Actually," she said softly, "there is one more thing I need before we head back to the party."

He gazed down into her eyes, which were lit by the moonlight that streamed over them in their private rose-filled hideaway. "Anything," he said again, even though he already knew what she was going to do. What she was going to say. Because he knew her better than anyone else in the world. Just as she knew him. "Tell me, and I'll give it to you."

She stepped out of his arms just enough to be able to reach for the zipper on her dress that ran between her breasts. "I need you to love me," she said at the exact moment that she pulled it down. "Here. Tonight. It's always been you, Ryan. *Always.*"

And as he laid her down on the bench beneath the moon and the stars, surrounded by roses and grape-vines, to love her sweet and hot all at the same time, Ryan hated to think what his life would have been like without Vicki.

Thank God, he'd never have to find out.

CHAPTER SEVEN

Flowers of every color and scent spilled from pots on the large stone patio that overlooked the vineyards where Zach and Ryan waited. Neither man looked at all anxious about getting married. On the contrary, it was clear to every one of the hundreds of wedding guests that the brothers were nearly out of patience as they waited for their brides to appear.

"Hopefully, the girls will be out here soon," Sophie whispered to Lori.

"No kidding," Lori agreed. "Otherwise our brothers look like they're going to go caveman."

Maybe Mary shouldn't have laughed in agreement as she stood at the front with her oldest son, Marcus, to co-officiate the wedding. But her children had always been her greatest joy—and watching each of them find love meant everything to her.

The first notes of the *Wedding March* rang out through the vineyard, and Mary's chest squeezed. In a matter of minutes, her sons would be pledging their hearts to the women they loved. And she'd have two new daughters. She couldn't wait, her smile growing even wider as Heather emerged from a rose-covered archway.

Zach's indrawn breath easily carried to Mary's ears as he saw his bride in her gown for the very first time. Heather was absolutely radiant in white silk that draped elegantly over her curves. The designer had made her the perfect dress—simple, yet breathtaking.

As she walked up the aisle on her father's arm, Heather never once took her eyes from Zach. Mary swore she could feel the connection between them, so strong that no one, and nothing, would ever break it. Even when Heather's father kissed his daughter's cheek before moving back to his seat, Heather held Zach's gaze. And when Zach reached for her hand and kissed it, Mary nearly broke into sobs right then and there.

It suddenly hit her: How on earth was she ever going to make it through not just one of her children's weddings—but two on the very same day—without falling completely apart?

There was barely enough time for the crowd to catch its collective breath before Vicki emerged from beneath an arch made of baseball bats held by Ryan's teammates.

But it wasn't just the bride's unique entrance that

had Mary smiling. It was seeing how bright Vicki's eyes were, how flushed her cheeks, as she smiled at her groom. Ryan's grin nearly split his face as he took in the stunning vision of his best friend, dressed all in white.

Never had two brides been more beautiful, each in their own special way. Where Heather's gown was pure simplicity, Vicki's made you look once, twice, then again. Yes, there was white silk and lace, but instead of using thread to connect the fabrics, zippers crisscrossed to create a corset-like bodice that was positively breathtaking.

Pure joy infused every step Vicki took toward Ryan on her father's arm. Mary's son didn't wait for them to make it all the way to the altar, but met them halfway down the aisle. Vicki's father laughed along with everyone else at the groom's enthusiasm, and once her father had hugged his daughter with tears in his eyes, Ryan took his bride into his arms and kissed her soundly, long before any vows were spoken. When they finally drew apart, they walked hand in hand to stand beside Zach and Heather in front of the guests.

Marcus moved forward to begin the ceremony. "Thank you for coming today to celebrate the love between Heather and Zach *and* Vicki and Ryan. My mother and I are honored that they asked us to officiate their double wedding today."

Mary had to take a deep breath to steady her emotions before moving to Marcus's side. Smiling first at the brides and grooms, she then looked out over the large group of beloved family and friends on the patio. "As you can see, we decided to do things a little differently this time." The crowd laughed, and she continued, saying, "In addition to having two weddings today, we also thought we'd have some nontraditional ring bearers be a part of the wedding. Please welcome Atlas and Cuddles."

Still holding Zach's hand, Heather turned and gave a low whistle. A few moments later, Atlas and Cuddles began to trot down the aisle, the wedding bands tied with ribbons to their collars.

Seeing the two dogs together—one huge, one tiny—never failed to make Mary smile. Three hundred people obviously agreed as applause rang out. Heather and Zach had trained their dogs so well that clapping and laughter didn't distract them from their task as they continued to walk up the aisle.

Just then, out of the corner of her eye, Mary saw a flash of golden fur near where she and Marcus were standing at the upper edge of the patio. When Atlas's ears perked up, Mary guessed the Great Dane must have seen it too. Always alert to her dog's behavior, Heather gave another whistle to keep his focus on her.

But a moment later, when another golden streak of

fur shot by, before anyone could stop the teacup Yorkie, Cuddles was off and chasing the rabbit. Atlas was one of the most well trained dogs Mary had ever come across, but how could anyone expect him not to dash off after his best friend and two rabbits?

Zach cursed softly, then quickly kissed Heather and said, "I'll go get them." He was gone in a flash, in his suit, chasing the two dogs.

"I'll help," Ryan said. After a kiss for his bride, he was running out into the vineyard too.

Again, Mary knew she shouldn't laugh, but seeing her two sons in their perfectly pressed wedding suits yelling for the dogs as they ran between rows of vines was something she knew she'd never forget.

"I should probably go help them, shouldn't I?" Marcus said, amusement threading each word.

Through the laughter she was barely holding in, Mary agreed with her eldest son. "Probably. Especially since it looks like Smith, Chase, and Gabe are all already heading out in search of the dogs."

"I would go too," Lori said, "but I'm wearing heels."

"You can do absolutely *anything* in heels," Sophie noted.

Though it was true, Lori shot back, "I don't exactly see you running out there to help, Soph."

Sophie grinned at her twin. "That's because I can

barely keep from falling over in my heels even on solid ground." She looked at Heather and Vicki next. "But if you want me to try, I can join my brothers out there. And I'll make Lori come too."

Fortunately, neither bride looked overly upset by what had happened. "Atlas and Cuddles will grow tired of chasing the rabbits soon, and then they'll come back," Heather replied. "At least, I hope they will."

Vicki grinned at Heather. "We can always do the ceremony without the rings, and later, when the dogs are done having fun, we can slip the rings on."

Fortunately, a great *whoop* rang out from the vines. "We've got 'em!" one of the men called out.

Zach and Ryan emerged from the vines a few moments later, victorious heroes with Cuddles safely in Zach's arms and Atlas walking calmly beside Ryan. Seeing that neither dog was wearing a ribbon anymore, Mary hoped the rings were safely in the grooms' pockets. Their brothers fanned out behind them, and Mary swore she heard a collective sigh from the female guests at seeing so many Sullivan men together like this.

As if they'd choreographed it, both grooms stepped back up onto the terrace and pulled the rings out of their pockets to hold them up like trophies to their brides. While the crowd continued to laugh, Heather and Vicki petted the dogs and kissed their men.

Finally, the ceremony could begin.

Again.

Neither Zach nor Ryan looked perfectly pressed anymore, but as far as Mary was concerned, it was exactly right for her car-racing and ball-playing sons. They were both just as active and energetic as their father, and somewhere, some way, she knew Jack was watching today's wedding, laughing right along with her at how much fun it all was—and tearing up with her too.

* * *

"Thank you for bringing the dogs back," Heather whispered into Zach's ear while he held her tightly. He wished they could say their vows just like this, without his ever needing to let her go.

"They did it on purpose, you know," he whispered back. "Cuddles's sense of humor is definitely rubbing off on Atlas."

She didn't deny that it was true, simply laughed softly as she held him just as tightly. "Our two big goofballs."

"Soon to be three," he said through the lump in his throat at the thought of the new baby they were going to have.

Marcus cleared his throat. "Looks like it's time to get this show on the road, for real this time."

Zach gave Heather one more kiss before they reluctantly drew apart. Reaching for each other's hands, they were staring into each other's eyes as Marcus began the ceremony.

"Heather and Zach, we are gathered here today to witness your love for each other." Marcus focused on Zach. "Zach, one of the reasons you always do so well on the race track is that you have an innate sense of how to make the right decisions in a split second, even when your life is on the line. We all agree that the best decision you ever made was to fall in love with Heather—and to continue pursuing her until she fell in love with you too." Marcus turned to Heather. "Heather, you're everything we could hope for in a new sister. Strong. Courageous. Fun. And, best of all, willing to put up with our brother." He grinned at both of them. "Now, for what we've all been waiting for— your vows to each other." Marcus stepped back so that Zach and Heather were the sole focus of the guests.

"Heather, until I met you, I sped through life, thinking I needed to experience everything before it was too late." Zach had always been as cool as they came, but right now his throat was so tight with emotion that he had to work to get the words out. "But the only thing I would have missed, truly missed, was you." He squeezed her hands tighter and would have pulled her closer, but she'd already taken a step toward him, obviously needing the same thing. "You've been mine since the first moment I set eyes on you. And I'm yours. Always." Zach took the wedding band from his pocket and slipped it onto the third finger of her left hand.

Tears were spilling down her cheeks as she gazed from the ring into his eyes. Lifting their hands where they were linked, he gently brushed the wetness away.

"Zach." Heather's voice trembled, even just saying his name, and he loved her more than ever as she smiled at him through her tears of joy. "I never believed forever was possible until you. And I never thought anyone could break through my walls either. But then, there you were. The man I secretly dreamed of. Someone strong enough to love me even when it wasn't easy. Even when I was scared by what I was feeling." They both moved closer again, so that he could practically taste each of her words as she said, "The dogs fell for you first, but it didn't take me long to realize they were right. I am yours, just as you are mine. And I'll love you forever." She took the ring he handed her and slipped it on his left hand as she said again, "Forever."

Everyone in the crowd was sniffling when Marcus spoke again. "Zach, Heather, by the power vested in me by the state of California, I now pronounce you husband and wife."

Neither Zach nor Heather had any plans of waiting until Marcus gave them leave to kiss to seal their vows. And though every one of their kisses had been beyond hot for the past three years, their first kiss as husband and wife truly was special. Not only hot, not only perfect, but a promise they were making to each other to never give up and never let go. No matter what.

Because their love was meant to last forever.

★ ★ ★

Ryan smiled at Vicki as she wiped away her tears from watching Heather and Zach say their vows. He'd known this would be a deeply emotional wedding— but as far as he was concerned, that only made it better.

Ever since he'd come back from chasing down the dogs, he'd been holding her in his arms. Now, he whispered, "Ready for it to be our turn?"

There were no more shadows, no more lingering hurt in her eyes, as she nodded. "I can't wait another second."

He didn't know who kissed whom then—just that it was the perfect way to begin their own ceremony.

Ryan's mother moved to stand before them, her smile warm and full of great love. "Vicki and Ryan, we couldn't be more thrilled about being here with you today. You two have loved each other for so many years, and I can't remember ever being happier than I am right now, knowing you are finally going to become husband and wife." His mother was one of the strongest people he knew, but her eyes were damp as she said, "And now, we can't wait to hear your vows." When his mother stepped back, it felt to Ryan as if he and Vicki were the only two people in the world.

"Vicki." Ryan wanted to freeze-frame this moment, wanted to remember every detail. "We were fifteen years old when you saved my life—and then became my best friend." He lifted their joined hands to his chest. "You're the most important person in the world to me, and I vow to do anything and everything I can to make you happy from this moment forward." He slipped the wedding band on the ring finger of her left hand. "I love you, Vicki. More than you'll ever know."

His beautiful, glowing bride threw her arms around him and held on tight. But her tears weren't the only ones falling—his were too. He'd waited so damned long for this moment, he almost couldn't believe it was finally here.

Finally, Vicki drew back. Her cheeks were still streaked with tears, but her voice was strong as she reached for his hands again and said, "You make me so happy, Ryan. You're my best friend. You're my one and only love. You're the first person I want to see when I wake up in the morning. You're the one I want to share absolutely everything with all day long. And you're the man I want to fall asleep with each night, knowing I'm perfectly, wonderfully safe in your arms." Her lips curved up into a stunning smile that made his heart flip around in his chest as she slid his wedding band into place on his left hand. "It's always been you. And it always will be. I love you."

Mary stepped up to say, "By the power vested in me by the state of California, I now pronounce you husband and wife," but Ryan and Vicki were kissing before his mother finished speaking.

It had taken nearly two decades to win Vicki as his wife. And now, Ryan couldn't wait for all the decades in front of them as two halves of the whole they'd always been—and always would be.

CHAPTER EIGHT

Marcus's wife, Nicola, Mia's husband, Ford Vincent, and their friend Drew Morrison took the stage not long after the ceremony to sing a beautiful song that Nicola and Ford had written for the happy couples. Mary overheard more than one guest say, after listening to the three world-famous stars perform, that this had to be the wedding of the century.

Perhaps she was biased, but she couldn't help but agree. Not only because the two couples were meant to be—but because everyone in the family had come together to help in some way. Yet again, Mary gave thanks for the day she'd met Jack Sullivan in downtown San Francisco. He'd changed her life in the best possible ways—first with his love and then by giving her eight incredible kids.

After eating their fill of the delicious meal, everyone took to the dance floor, and Mary was dancing with her brother-in-law William Sullivan. "I know I say this every single time," she commented as they swayed together, "but this has been an absolutely perfect wedding, hasn't it?"

He smiled as he took in the same beautiful family picture—kids and dogs and happy couples all around them. "It sure is. I just wish my brother could be here today. Jack would be so proud of how you raised your kids, and how they're raising theirs."

She swallowed past the lump in her throat, something she'd had a lot of practice doing for the past twenty-plus years. Not just because she still missed Jack so very much, but also because William hadn't had an easy time of it either. He'd once been a talented and extremely famous painter, with a wife he adored beyond reason and four children. But thirty years ago, things had gone off course for William. So far off course that his wife had walked out on the family and taken her own life. William hadn't painted in thirty years, and his relationship with his kids had often been fractured as well, but Mary knew he was doing what he could to try to fix things.

"You're not doing too bad yourself, you know," she encouraged him in a gentle voice. "Your kids are just as extraordinary as mine."

Drake was a renowned painter, Suzanne was a brilliant computer programmer with a thriving tech company in Manhattan, Harrison was an expert in medieval history at Columbia University, and Alec owned a very lucrative business building private planes just outside of New York City.

William looked extremely proud—but somewhat anxious too—as he looked over at his children. "I know they are. Despite their father."

"William." Mary put her hand on her brother-in-law's face, one that was similar enough to her late husband's to make her heart twinge every time she looked at him. William had lost his wife not long after she'd given birth to Drake, their youngest. Thirty years later, Mary could see that the five of them were still reeling from what that loss had done to their family. For so long, she'd hoped they could heal what was broken. She still did. She told her brother-in-law yet again, "Whatever you need, whatever your kids need, you're not in this alone. You have me. You have all of us."

She could see how close to the surface his emotion was as William nodded. "I know." He forced a smile for her. "It's always good to be reminded, though."

Mary was about to say something more when she suddenly heard a gasp from behind her. Dylan and Grace had been dancing—with both Mason and Grace's very large pregnant belly between them—but now they were standing still in the middle of the crowd.

With so many children and grandchildren of her

own, Mary had seen this look enough times to guess what had just happened. "Grace, honey?"

Grace's eyes were big as she said, "My water just broke."

As if her words had been broadcast over a loud-speaker, several of Dylan's siblings quickly gathered around their brother and his wife, with Dylan's parents, Claudia and Max, getting there first. Mary smiled as she and William moved back on the dance floor to let them all in.

Mary's sister-in-law Claudia put her arm around Grace. "Have you started having any contractions yet?"

"I've had quite a few Braxton-Hicks cramps over the past week, so I figured that was all they were today too. Especially since I'm still two weeks away from my due date."

Grace and Dylan had Mason already, so Grace wasn't a novice to childbirth. Still, the second baby often had a way of coming faster than you expected.

"How far apart are your contractions?" Claudia asked.

Grace opened her mouth to answer, then winced instead as another contraction hit her. "Maybe two, three minutes," she finally replied.

Dylan looked stunned. "If I'd known you were in labor this whole time—"

Now that the pain had passed, Grace calmly put

her hand on her husband's cheek and said, "I didn't even know. And I've done this bef—" She hadn't quite gotten out the full sentence before another contraction hit.

"That's a heck of a lot faster than two minutes," Dylan's sister, Mia, noted.

"Marcus, Nicola," Ford, Mia's husband, called out, "we're going to need a doctor."

"I'm already on hold with the hospital." Nicola moved closer, a cell phone up to her ear. "They've just paged the on-call doctor. And Marcus is getting a bedroom ready." She grinned at Grace and Dylan. "This is so exciting! Why don't I take you both inside?"

"Mommy"—Mason tugged at Grace's skirt—"are you going to have the baby now?"

Dylan lifted his little boy up and smooched him on the cheek. "We sure are."

"Yes!" Mason pumped his fist. He clearly couldn't wait to be a big brother. "It's taken *forever*."

Tatiana Landon, Ian's fiancée, held out her arms to the little boy. "How about we spend some time having fun together while your mommy and daddy make a beautiful baby brother or sister for you?"

Just because Tatiana was one of the biggest movie stars in the world didn't mean she cared one whit about a toddler getting her dress dirty or wrinkled. Neither did Dylan's brother Ian. Becoming a billionaire hadn't changed him—he'd always been a great, and protective, older brother.

"Aunt Mary, Uncle William," Dylan said, "could you let Rafe, Brooke, Adam, and Kerry know we'd love for them to come up to the house when you see them?"

"Of course, Dylan." Mary gave her nephew a hug. He'd met Grace and baby Mason when she had come to interview him for a feature in a boating magazine. It had been love at first sight for all three of them.

Mason went happily into Tatiana's arms as Grace and Dylan headed into the house to meet the physician who was on the way. Claudia, Max, Mia, and Ford followed them into the house to help with anything they might need during labor.

Rafe and Brooke came dashing up a few minutes later, with Adam and Kerry close behind.

"We heard Grace went into labor." Brooke looked beyond thrilled by the news.

"Is there anything we can do to help?" her husband, Rafe, asked.

Mary thought Brooke and Rafe were utterly sweet together. They'd grown up spending summers next door to each other on a lake in the Pacific Northwest—two kids who had no idea that one day they'd meet again as adults and fall head over heels in love with each other.

"Everything's under control," Mary let them know. "They've already got a full crew in Marcus and Nicola's house, although Dylan would like to have all of you nearby so that you can meet the baby as soon as he or she is born."

"I've been to literally hundreds of weddings," Kerry Dromoland said, smiling widely with Adam's arm tight around her waist, "and I have to say this one is now my all-time favorite."

Kerry was one of the top wedding planners on the West Coast—and though Adam had once sworn he'd never fall in love and get married, Mary knew he'd move mountains for his fiancée.

"Let's head into the house." Adam grinned as he added, "Hopefully, there's still time to convince them to name the new baby after one of us."

Ethan Sullivan, another of Jack's brothers, moved beside Mary and William. "You really know how to put on a wedding." Ethan had settled in Maine several decades ago and had six great kids of his own. Mary's kids always loved hanging out with their East Coast cousins whenever they could get together.

Mary grinned at Ethan, then William. "I hope both of you are taking notes. Because something tells me you're both going to be in the thick of it in the not-so-distant future."

She barely managed to hold back her laughter at

the look Jack's brothers gave each other—something akin to panic on their handsome faces.

"We're still a long way off," Ethan said.

"So are we," William agreed.

This time, Mary didn't bother to contain her laughter. "Famous last words."

She turned to look at their big, wonderful family. Sullivans had come from every corner of the world to celebrate today's double wedding. Mary didn't know who would be the next to find love. All she knew was that when true love came for each of her nieces and nephews in New York and Maine, even if the road to *forever* wasn't always an easy one, finding the person they were meant to be with would definitely change their lives in the best possible ways.

And even though she couldn't help but tease her brothers-in-law, she knew they'd both do great. Because they loved their children with everything they were.

Lori and Grayson moved into the group. "Isn't this great?" Lori said. "We've never had a baby born at a wedding before." She smiled at Mary. "I wonder where we'll be when ours is ready to pop?"

Mary held her breath as she looked from her daughter to her son-in-law. "Are you..."

Lori threw herself into her mother's arms. "I am!" She was positively glowing as Mary kissed her cheek and then Grayson's. After William and Ethan did the same, Lori said, "I didn't want to take the spotlight off anyone else today, but we just can't keep the news to ourselves anymore." Grayson put his arms around her from behind and she held on tight to her husband as she said, "I can't wait to have a little boy or girl in seven months. Or maybe even both, like Soph."

At last, Mary finally fell apart. She was just so *happy*. Overjoyed from the top of her head to the tips of her toes. There were more hugs, and more tears of joy, and she'd barely managed to dry her tears when Dylan burst through the patio doors.

"We have a new baby boy!" Cheers went up from the guests as Dylan scooped up Mason from where he was playing jacks with Tatiana and Ian. "Let's go meet your new brother. His name is Aaron."

With new tears in her eyes, Mary took William's and Ethan's hands. "What do you say we go celebrate on the dance floor?"

New marriages. New life. Family laughing and celebrating together in the Napa Valley sunshine.

It truly had been the best wedding ever.

And, she thought with a smile, she couldn't wait until the next one…

★ ★ ★ ★ ★

~ A special THANK YOU from Bella Andre ~

If you are already a fan of the Sullivans, I hope you loved getting to be a part of the double-wedding magic and reconnecting with all your favorites! If you are just getting started with the series, you can find out how Zach and Heather first found love in IF YOU WERE MINE and learn more about Ryan and Vicki's love story in LET ME BE THE ONE.

As a special bonus, I've put together a behind-the-scenes look at what inspired me to first write about the Sullivans—and why I plan to keep writing about them for as long as I possibly can! Just to go www. BellaAndre.com/Secret to find out more.

Now that the San Francisco and Seattle Sullivans have all found love, it's time for their cousins in New York and Maine to find love too! Drake Sullivan kicks off the New York branch with NOW THAT I'VE FOUND YOU and his sister, Suzanne, will be next in SINCE I FELL FOR YOU!

Thank you for reading my books and for sending me such lovely emails and comments online. Knowing that you love my Sullivans as much as I do means everything to me!

~ Bella Andre ~

★ ★ ★ ★ ★

For news on upcoming books, sign up for Bella Andre's New Release Newsletter: BellaAndre.com/Newsletter

ABOUT THE AUTHOR

Having sold more than 5 million books, Bella Andre's novels have been #1 bestsellers around the world and have appeared on the *New York Times* and *USA Today* bestseller lists 30 times. She has been the #1 Ranked Author on a top 10 list that included Nora Roberts, JK Rowling, James Patterson and Steven King, and Publishers Weekly named Oak Press (the publishing company she created to publish her own books) the Fastest-Growing Independent Publisher in the US. After signing a groundbreaking 7-figure print only deal with Harlequin MIRA, Bella's "The Sullivans" series has been released in paperback in the US, Canada, and Australia.

Known for "sensual, empowered stories enveloped in heady romance" (Publishers Weekly), her books have been Cosmopolitan Magazine "Red Hot Reads" twice and have been translated into ten languages. Winner of the Award of Excellence, The Washington Post called her "One of the top writers in America" and she has been featured by Entertainment Weekly, NPR, USA Today, Forbes, The Wall Street Journal, and TIME Magazine. A graduate of Stanford University, she has given keynote speeches at publishing conferences from Copenhagen to

Berlin to San Francisco, including a standing-room-only keynote at Book Expo America in New York City.

Bella also writes the New York Times bestselling Four Weddings and a Fiasco series as Lucy Kevin. Her "sweet" contemporary romances also include the USA Today bestselling Walker Island series written as Lucy Kevin.

If not behind her computer, you can find her reading her favorite authors, hiking, swimming or laughing. Married with two children, Bella splits her time between the Northern California wine country and a 100 year old log cabin in the Adirondacks.

For a complete listing of books, as well as excerpts and contests, and to connect with Bella:

Sign up for Bella's newsletter:
BellaAndre.com/Newsletter

Visit Bella's website at:
www.BellaAndre.com

Follow Bella on Twitter at:
twitter.com/bellaandre

Join Bella on Facebook at:
facebook.com/bellaandrefans

Follow Bella on Instagram:
instagram.com/bellaandrebooks

54556106R00064

Made in the USA
Lexington, KY
20 August 2016